Gramma, Grampa, and the Three Bears

To Hayse and Whister
Thank you for Loving
and respecting wild life —

Written by Jack Day
Illustrated by Rose Toth

Rose Toth

Jack Day

ISBN: 0615540570
ISBN 13: 9780615540573
Library of Congress Control Number: 2011938826
Jack Day Publishing, Bozeman, MT

Gramma, Grampa, and the Three Bears

Written by Jack Day

Dedication:

This book is dedicated to all of my kids, grandkids and my great grandchild, who all love to read and/or be read to.

Acknowledgements:

I thank my good friend Jane Quinn of 'Quilting in the Country' for encouraging me to embark on this little project. I also am appreciative of the many friends who read the original manuscript and offered their suggestions for improvement. I'm especially thankful to my best friend, partner and spouse, Karen, for all of her support.

A special tip of the hat goes out to Rose Toth whose wonderful illustrations bring the story to life. Also, kudos to my project team at CreateSpace.com for their creativity and professionalism in getting this endeavor off the ground.

Table of Contents:

Introduction

Gramma and Grampa's Backyard

Gramma and Grampa live in a house with lots of windows, just outside of town and very close to the mountains. The house stands on the side of a hill, so that the front of the house is much higher than the back. They have a very big back yard with many apple and plum trees. They also have a vegetable garden and some cherry trees. Because they have so much food in their yard, deer visit them almost every day. Last week a large five-point buck has been coming to feed.

Every year in the early fall, after the first frost, and when the apples have ripened, Gramma and Grampa are visited by beautiful black bears.

They have come to feed on all of the stuff that hasn't been picked. They really like the apples, but their most favorite food of all are the plums.

This year, Gramma and Grampa were really lucky to have a mamma bear and her two cubs spend a few weeks with them. This is a story about all of the fun that they had.

Chapter 1

Wow! The Cubs Find a Garbage Can

Gramma and Grampa sleep in a bedroom that is above their garage. It has a big window that looks out over the driveway. They keep their garbage can near the garage door. One night while they were asleep, a huge racket outside the window suddenly woke them up. Grampa jumped from the bed and ran over to the window to see what all the ruckus was about. When he looked down, he noticed that the lid was off the garbage container.

Grampa asked Gramma to come over to help him see what was going on. When their eyes got used to seeing in the dark, they noticed that the mamma bear had parked herself near the can. But where in the world were the two cubs?

Gramma and Grampa kept hearing all of this thrashing around, but they didn't know where it was coming from. Suddenly, the garbage can began bouncing around. And then it began wiggling back and forth. Finally, it tipped one way and then the other until it fell over on its side. Out rolled the two cubs. One had a banana peel over his ear, and the other had a piece of piecrust stuck to his rump.

Well, Grampa thought that this whole affair really scared the cubs, because they both scampered across the front lawn and hid in the bushes. Meanwhile, Mamma Bear just shook her head, as if to say, "Cubs will be cubs," and waddled off after them.

Chapter 2

Dancing Bears

Gramma and Grampa decided to keep their garbage can inside the garage so that the bears wouldn't be able to get in the container again. That meant they had to park the car in the driveway. You can guess what happened then.

A few nights later Gramma and Grampa were comfortably asleep under a soft down blanket. All of a sudden Grampa was awakened by a noise out in the driveway. Now, what could that be? Grampa shook Gramma awake and they ran over to the window to see what was going on. A full moon was shining brightly. The first thing they saw was Mamma Bear standing on her hind legs clapping her paws together.

The next thing they saw were the two cubs on the hood of the car dancing up a storm. They were bouncing up and down and turning in circles to the rhythm of their mother's clapping. Finally, the two cubs climbed down, and all three ambled off toward the hedges at the side of the yard.

The next morning Grampa went out to check the car to see if any damage was done. All he saw on the hood were the footprints of two happy, dancing bears.

Chapter 3

Piles and Piles of Poop

Gramma and Grampa took a long weekend trip to see the wild elk, bison, and wolves in Yellowstone National Park. It was a fun weekend, and they saw many wild animals.

When they arrived back home they went into their backyard to see if their friends, the bears, were still hanging around. They found a few broken branches on the plum trees where the bears had climbed to pick the fruit. They also found piles and piles of bear poop.

Now, even if you've never seen bear poop before, you will still be able to recognize it. It usually is in a pretty soft pile and has lots of undigested seeds and fruit pits in it. And, boy, it sure does stink.

Gramma and Grampa cleaned up the broken branches and filled a big trash bag with all of the poop. Now, they would be able to rake the leaves.

Chapter 4

The Cubs Take a Nap

Gramma and Grampa raked the leaves into big piles. Then they went into the house to have a good lunch of soup and sandwiches. They decided to eat in the sunroom. It is one of their favorite places to sit, because they could watch all of the birds and other animals that visit their backyard. While they were eating, Gramma spotted the mamma bear and her two cubs climbing over the fence into the yard.

What were they up to now? Well, the two cubs began rolling in the leaf piles. Then they scattered the leaves all over the place and threw them up in the air. They played and played until they were so tired that they had to lie down to take a nap. By the time they were finished playing, you would never have known that Gramma and Grampa had raked up the leaves.

In the meantime, Mamma Bear watched her cubs from a short distance away in the shadow of the shrubs. Grampa hoped that she had as much fun watching them play as he and Gramma did.

15

Chapter 5

Surprise for the Roofer

Gramma and Grampa usually sit in the sunroom and drink a cup of coffee early in the morning. Just beyond the big window, there are three huge pine trees that are right up against their neighbors' house.

One morning, while they were drinking their coffee, the three bears came marching down the backyard. They climbed over a fence and went to the pine trees. The mamma bear made the two cubs climb high up into the tree closest to the neighbors' house. Then she climbed up into the same tree. After a lot of wiggling around, they all settled down for a nice long sleep.

The next day the three bears did the same thing. They spent the whole day up in the tree resting. Even when Grampa went in the yard to rake the leaves again, they didn't budge.

On the third day, they climbed up into the tree once again. The cubs went first and then Mamma. Gramma decided that the mamma bear must have thought that was the best way that she could protect her two cubs.

About an hour after the bears had all settled down for their sleep, Gramma and Grampa noticed a roof repairman carrying a ladder into the front yard of the neighbors' house. He put up the ladder, picked up his tools, and climbed onto the roof. He walked across the roof toward the pine trees, whistling a happy tune.

He must have heard the mamma bear growl, because, suddenly, he looked up. And there he was staring right into the eyes of that big bear.

Well, he was really startled. His eyes almost popped out of his head. His face turned a ghostly white, and his hair, what there was of it, stood on end.

He threw his hands up in the air, scattering his tools all over the roof. Stumbling backward, he turned and ran for the ladder. He jumped on the ladder so hard that it tipped over. He and the ladder went crashing into the bushes below. Grampa knew the roofer was okay because he heard him jump into his truck, start the engine, and roar down the road.

Meanwhile, Mamma Bear let out a soft growl and closed her eyes, knowing she was doing a good job of protecting her young cubs.

Chapter 6

The Bears Go Visiting

Gramma and Grampa noticed the bears did not show up the next morning. Maybe they were tired of hanging around their yard. So they decided to drive to the grocery store to stock up on food for the next week.

As they approached the intersection of their road and another, they noticed that several cars were parked along the street. They saw people walking down the sidewalk. Gramma thought maybe one of the neighbors was having a birthday party.

They drove on to the grocery store and did the shopping. When they were finished they headed back toward their home. As they arrived at that same intersection, Grampa noticed that there were many more cars and trucks parked along the roads. There was a large crowd of people looking out into a nearby field.

So Gramma and Grampa parked the car and walked over to see what all of the commotion was about. You can imagine their surprise when they saw the bears perched in a bare Aspen tree, like three very big birds. The tree was next to a beautiful stream, a safe distance away from all the people.

More and more people kept showing up to get a look at the bears. It was causing a traffic jam. Eventually, the police arrived to control the traffic. Then the forest rangers came to make sure that no one got too close to the bear family. Finally, the local newspaper sent a photographer and a reporter to cover this big event. The photographer got busy taking photos with his camera with a huge telescopic lens. The reporter interviewed many of the people that came to see Gramma and Grampa's friends, the bears.

The next morning, right there on the front page of the newspaper, was a big picture of Mamma Bear and her two cubs sitting in the tree. There was also a story about the bears with lots of interviews included in the article. Gramma and Grampa's three bears were sure famous.

Chapter 7

Time to Say Goodbye

Gramma and Grampa tucked themselves into bed that night thinking that the three bears were so famous they probably would not come back to their yard. After they had been asleep for a couple of hours, Leo, the cat, suddenly jumped off the bed and ran to the door that leads out to the backyard from the bedroom.

Well, Gramma got out of bed to see what was going on. Then she called to Grampa to come over to the door and take a look. The two cubs were right there with their noses and paws pressed against the glass of the door. The mamma bear sat a couple of feet behind them, as calm as could be.

Gramma and Grampa believe that the bears came to thank them for all of the food from the yard and to say good-bye. They knew that it was time for them to head back to the mountains, to find their den, and to settle down for a long winter's sleep.

Gramma and Grampa used their knuckles to tap at the cubs' noses through the glass to let them know how much fun they had watching them throughout the fall.

The three bears slowly turned and waddled up the yard in the moonlight. In a few moments they were out of sight.

The End